finn's
thin book of
IRISH IRONIES

D0900954

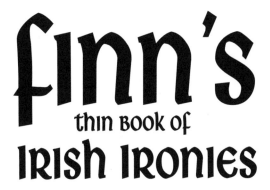

finn's
thin book of
Irish Ironies

By Patrick Watson

Illustrated By AISLIN and Mary Hughson

McArthur & Company
Toronto

First published in Canada in 2010 by
McArthur & Company
322 King Street West, Suite 402
Toronto, Ontario
M5V 1J2
www.mcarthur-co.com

Library and Archives Canada Cataloguing in Publication

Watson, Patrick, 1929-

   Finn's thin book of Irish ironies / by Patrick Watson ; illustrated by
Aislin and Mary Hughson.

Poems.
ISBN 978-1-55278-847-9

   1. Ireland--Poetry. I. Aislin II. Hughson, Mary III. Title.

PS8595.A85F56 2010   C811'.54   C2010-900577-5

The publisher would like to acknowledge the financial support of the Gov-
ernment of Canada through the Canada Book Fund and the Canada Council for our publishing activities. The publisher further wishes to acknowledge
the financial support of the Ontario Arts Council and the OMDC for our
publishing program.

Design and composition by Szol Design
Printed in Canada by Transcontinental

10 9 8 7 6 5 4 3 2 1

With thanks to professor Roy Foster, at Oxford, whose *History of Modern Ireland*, and *Life of W. B. Yeats* were a huge resource, and whose letter of encouragement when I sent him some sample lines early on was inspirational.

–Patrick Watson

Maeve Binchy and Gordon Snell in Dalkey
John and Mary Gallagher in Donegal
Jack Houlden, our driver in Dublin

–Aislin and Mary Hughson

Contents

x

PREFACE

A few years ago I picked up a copy of Tim Severin's 1979 book *The Brendan Voyage* in a second-hand shop in Ireland, left it lying around the house for months, finally settled into it one afternoon . . . and couldn't put it down. And the morning after I finished it I woke up with a poem about Brendan, almost finished, in my head.

> St. Brendan sailed the ocean
> With another monk or two –
> Or four, afloat in a leather boat
> Like some big old canoe . . . .(etc.)

I liked the verse well enough to scribble it down, in pencil, on a slip that lay in the bedside table drawer for months, maybe a couple of years, but when recovered (and by then I had been reading a lot of Irish history) looked good enough to suggest more. And when an early sharing of the work-in-progress with Terry Mosher (Aislin) led to his proposing to illustrate them, the momentum blossomed, I began to imagine myself a fictional Irish mythologist, Finn, and to be muttering away, new lines and themes, day after day.

And so here they are: *Finn's Thin Book (*and they have been received very well, when recited aloud in public or at parties). And Terry and Mary's illustrations are a superb enrichment of the whole.

Patrick Watson
Toronto, 2010

PART ONE

THE AGE of MYTH

THE VOYAGE OF ST. BRENDAN, (EARLY 6TH C.)

Saint Brendan sailed the ocean
With another monk or two,
(Or more) afloat in a leather boat
Like some big old canoe.
And if they came to Canada,
Or if they came to Maine,
They only stayed a week or so
And then sailed home again.

The legends tell of monsters
So fierce they'd make you faint,
And storms and icebergs out to kill
Our oceanic Saint.
But finally these fearless friars
Came home safe to Erin
Thus endin' Brendan's brief but brave
Adventures in seafarin'.

3

THE OGHAM GLYPHS

One Dr. Barry Fell announced
In 1983
He'd found some texts in West Virginia,
Knew they had to be
The work of Irish Christians,
Pre-Columbian, no doubt,
And as a world authority
Had worked their meaning out,

And scientists began to ask
Could this be evidence
That Brendan and his boys
Got this far south? Could it make sense?
Ah well, they found poor Fell was not
What he had claimed, the sod.
He'd done it as a cunning stunt
And it was a total fraud.

St. Patrick: 5ᵗʰ Century

Once back from Rome he walked the Boyne
To Tara, where he found
The Druid chief, King Laoighre
There in Tara's famous Mound.
Patrick baptized a Druid priest
While Laoighre, on a whim,
Would not convert but gave the Saint
A castle, down at Trim.

So now this Frenchman (well, a lad
From Gaul, almost the same),
Once just a slave but now a brave
And celebrated name,
Lived to be a hundred three
But finally grew weary
Of never knowing how you're really
S'posed to say "King Laoigrhe."

THE 9TH CENTURY MANUSCRIPTS

*T*he Dimma Gospels, *Lindisfarme,*
And, best, *The Book of Kells,*
The finest of all Celtic art
A mass of work that tells
How Irish monks and friars worked
Throughout the worst Dark Ages
To keep great books alive in these
Illuminated pages.

Not just the Gospels – they're best known
But great philosophy
And poetry and history
Through those black centuries.
With most of Europe in the grip
Of Odin, Mars and Ba'al
Those monks saved Civilization.
Read the book. It's by Tom Cahill.

EXPUNGED FROM THE
BOOK OF KELLS

priest,
a rabbi
and a mullah
met one night
in a shebeen...

"AISLIN"

THE FIRST IRISH COIN

Nine hundred ninety-seven,
Sitric, King of Dublin called
Upon his Royal Goldsmith,
Known as Mac Culháir the Bald
He said, "I have some ancient
Roman coins among my treasures,
And up to yesterday,
Although I've gazed on them with pleasure

I had not thought that Dublin ought
To have something just like 'em
Look, here's a sketch, and you're the wretch
Who's going to cast and strike 'em.
Let's try to keep the value high,
We mustn't make too many.
It's a soldier's pay for three whole days.
I'm calling it The Penny."

DUBLIN AND THE DANES, 1014 AD

Dublin's name means Black Pool.
It's on old Ptolemy's map.
Two centuries of Viking rule
Come after one cold snap
That hits the town with nonstop snow
For more than ninety days
And then the bloody Norseman comes
And builds, and breeds, and stays

Through battle after battle
Till one Brian, called Boru
Defeats them at Clontarf
With twenty thousand strong and true.
But some say those damn Danes might just
Have had the real last larff,
Since they hacked Boru to pieces
In that battle of Clontarf.

THE ONLY IRISH WITCH-BURNING, 1324

The Bishop of Kilkenny
Shared Pope John the twenty-second's
Obsessions about witchcraft
And so, because he reckoned
That Alice Kyteler had slept
With a demon named FitzArt,
He sentenced her to burn,
But Alice managed to depart

For England, where she vanished
Leaving Petronilla Midia,
A pal and fellow sorcerer
To take the rap *in sidia*.
They burned poor Petronilla first
Before decapitation
A rather grisly way to earn
A world-first reputation.

THE BATTLE OF KNOCKDOE, 1504

The nineteenth day of August, it was,
Fifteen-hundred four,
The young king Burke of Clanicard
Some twenty months before
Had taken Galway City.
Now Fitzgerald of Kildare
Came to take it back.
The greatest armies anywhere

Or ever seen in Ireland,
Ten thousand Irish men
Fought that day until Galway
Had changed hands once again.
One buck there brought a handgun
Irish warfare's first: admire it.
He used it for a bludgeon, 'cos
He didn't know how to fire it.

HUGH O'NEILL,
1550-1616

If O'Donnell was the sword
Of Ulster's new Confederation,
The brain was Hugh O'Neill,
The greatest soldier of the nation.
A wily buck, he trained and stuck
At first, with London's forces
Then picked the Royal pocket to buy
Men and guns and horses.

And he and Red O'Donnell
And Maguire, another Lord
Wiped out 5,000 English
At the blood-soaked Yellow Ford.
"The Monster" then, they called him
Much too friendly with the Spanish,
But it would cost them dearly
When they tried to make him vanish.

O'NEILL AND ESSEX, 1599

Elizabeth sent Essex out
To deal with The O'Neill
And he and Hugh, in public view
In water to their heels
Talked it out on horseback,
In the middle of the River.
And Essex never knew how Hugh
Induced him to deliver

Concessions that enraged the Queen,
Put Essex in the Tower,
Brought thousands more from Britain's shore
To shore up British power,
Brought bribery and treason
Swamped O'Neill and all his Rebels
And set in train the endless pain
We came to name "The Troubles."

THE BATTLE OF KINSALE, CHRISTMAS DAY, 1601

O'Neill, with Red O'Donnell
Marched south to fight Mountjoy
With some three thousand Spanish troops
Together they'd destroy
The British, down in Munster
And build a Great Alliance,
Dublin, Madrid, the Vatican
Maybe even France.

But in the end they botched it
With O'Neill too far ahead,
And Mountjoy's horsemen quite superb
And soon the fields ran red
With Irish blood and Spanish blood.
The Spanish soon set sail,
And left O'Neill destroyed there
At the Battle of Kinsale.

THE MOUNTJOY METHOD, 1602

Mountjoy as Lord Lieutenant
Chose starvation as the tool
To force the rebel Ulstermen
To yield to British rule.
So he destroyed their crops
And later sent some men around
Who came away in some dismay
To tell him what they'd found.

Three little children had for days
Been roasting their dead mum,
And eating, starting at her feet
And to her neck had come.
But Mountjoy frowned and thundered
"So! You'll take these wee ones hence
And hang them! Eating people
Is a Capital Offence."

IRISH TROOPS FOR HIRE: 1500-1800

In days of yore and long before
The paramilitaries
Irish soldiers fought on foreign shores
As mercenaries.
Bold, immune to cold,
Bad food, and even bad command,
They'd fight like mad for any flag,
They were in great demand.

French and Spanish princes
Who hired them a lot
Declared them taller, healthier,
Than Dane or Brit or Scot,
But many say the reason they
Fought bravely was in fact
Their relentless sense of humour,
What the Irish call "The Craic."

17

THE HARRYING OF MOILIN OG (16TH C.)

O'Donnell made his way around
The island stealing cows
That's how the chieftains did it then
And while it did arouse
A measure of resentment, it
Was really, at the base,
A form of rent, or tribute,
So you put on a good face.

But Hugh once knicked a few off Moilin
Og. He didn't know it
But Moilin was renowned in Ireland
Yes, he was a Poet.
And even Chiefs don't mess with them:
Hugh brought back two for one,
And Moilin made some poems, they drank,
Embraced, and it was done.

THE OCTOBER REBELLION, 1641

Another O'Neill, Owen Roe,
Became a star in Spain.
He fought the Seven Years War for them
And then came home again
To lead the Catholic rebels
Of October 23rd
In battle after battle
Till his finest, at Benburb:

Only 70 Catholics dead
While strewn across the field
Some 3,000 Puritans
(Whose wounds would never heal.)
But then while Owen drank the health
Of those he'd just defeated
He learned his Dublin pals
Had sold him out and signed a treaty.

9/11 (1649):
CROMWELL AT DROGHEDA

Of all the Irish ironies
That hang upon a name
There's none so wry as that cold guy
Who brought about the shame
Of Drogheda, his brutal army
Putting to the slaughter
The entire population,
Man and woman, son and daughter.

Except a few who made it through
And lived to tell how all
Their families were burned and stabbed
Or stood against a wall.
And shot, they cried. Cromwell denied it
Then began to hector
His critics, whereupon the Brits
Proclaimed him "Lord Protector."

Johnathan Swift, 1668-1745

With Gulliver's wit he gave a fit
To bullies and to prigs,
To Ireland's oppressors,
To bishops, Tories, Whigs.
He fought the debased coinage
And won – against the Brits,
And ended several poems with — get this:
"Celia, Celia shits!"

He modestly proposed
That eating babies be a cure
For the hideous starvation
That afflicted Ireland's poor.
When he rode down in Dublin Town
The Catholic streetfolk cheered him;
A Protestant! St. Patrick's Dean,
Their champion of freedom.

1685: Catholic Rules at Last, OK?

The Irish Catholics often looked
To France to keep alive
Their hopes. When England
Got a Catholic King, in '85
(James Two, the Stuart Fool)
He thought he could undo
The Protestant Supremacy
In just a year or two.

Tyrconnel, Lord Lieutenant now
Put Catholics everywhere:
The courts, the castle, even Catholic troops
In Berkeley Square!
And made a secret treaty
With France, by which he planned
To crown the French Louis XIV
As King of Ireland!

THE SWORD OF BISHOP WALKER
(D. JULY 1, 1690)

King Billy's Soldier/Bishop, Walker
Sword in hand did fall
At the Battle of the Boyne
And ever since, on Derry's wall,
His statue stood there, brandishing
That blade against the sky,
"For Ulster and for Liberty,"
The Unionists would cry.

Until in 1829
One sunny day in spring,
The Catholic Emancipation Act
Made church bells ring
From Donegal to Cork
And with a loud spontaneous clatter
Old Walker's blade, that very day
Mysteriously shattered.

THE ROTUNDA, 1745

It came out of the famine
Back in 1739
Bartholomew Mosse, an Army Surgeon then,
Saw women dying
Destitute and freezing,
In despair on every hand,
And suddenly decided
To found, for his home land,

A *Hospital for Lying-In*,
— We'd say 'Maternity' —
So Surgeon Mosse became
A male midwife, and shortly he
Moved it to its present site,
Where it got its new name
The first in all the world, they say,
To Dublin's lasting fame.

THE HEDGE SCHOOLS
(EARLY 18ᵀᴴ C.)

The century's just starting
When Dublin tells the schools
That teaching Roman Catholic doctrine
Is against the rules.
So those who can afford it
Set up secret schools outdoors –
For Irish history and tradition,
Catholic law and lore.

By 1826
A State Inquiry alleges
That 75 per cent of all
School kids are in the Hedges
A poet, Judge O'Hagan, wrote
"Stretched out on Mountain Fern
The teacher and his pupils meet
Feloniously to learn."

THE WHITEBOYS

Among the brave who stood up
For their rights, to the unjust –
(Landlords, and cruel priests
Among them) now we must discuss
Those groups of youths who fought abuse
Under some odd names.
Somehow *The Whiteboys* were the ones
Who earned the greatest fame,

They mostly worked in Wexford, but
It wasn't just the Whiteboys
Other counties had their Oatboys
Steelboys, even Rightboys.
They wrecked great houses, fences,
Scattered cows, committed arson
But far as we can tell they never killed
Or hurt a person.

Two teenagers · BELFAST

Stomping boots →

AISLIN 75

WOLFE TONE,
1763-1798

In cyberspace a Wolf Tone
Is a sound that's slightly ribald.
Two hundred years ago, my dears,
It was a buck called Theobald.
(It sounds sublime: observe the rhyme.)
He was the one who founded
The great United Irishmen.
For several years they hounded

The occupying Brits. The French
Helped out with expeditions
That landed troops in Mayo,
But failed in all their missions.
The Brits caught up with Tone
In '98, on one French boat,
And sent him down to Dublin town,
Where he cut his own sweet throat.

James Napper Tandy,
1740-1803

A tradesman's son, a friend of Tone,
A drunkard and a dandy
A passionate United Irishman,
Was Napper Tandy.
They came down hard on his Rebel Guard.
He fled across the ocean,
Then back to France to take his chances
With the Revolution.

He sealed his fate in '98
With French troops and a ship
He made landfall at Donegal,
Said, "Right lads: Let her rip!"
But they had to carry him back on board
His head so full of brandy
That Britain soon brought off the ruin
Of Jamey Napper Tandy.

31

THE UNITED IRISHMEN, 1798

It's really like a postscript
To the story of Wolfe Tone
But suddenly I realized
It's really not well known:
The movement that he put together,
Sudden and dramatic
Protestants and Catholics,
A republic, democratic.

And maybe if they hadn't brought
The bloody French ashore
(For England hated France)
They might have done a great deal more.
But now the Brits just hacked and burned
And slaughtered them until
The last one was wiped out,
In Wexford's town of Vinegar Hill.

PIRES-WEXFORD...

33

THE UNION,
(1798)

The Act of Union Britain tried
To make in '98
Was meant to end the bloodstained trend,
Instead it fanned the hate.
It took away the people's say,
Killed Dublin's Parliament,
And disenfranchised millions.
A message had been sent:

London Rules O.K!
If Ireland ever had been one,
Now Ulstermen fought Orangemen,
The nobles cursed the Crown,
Peasants and landlords went to war,
And all this set the stage
For a great new Catholic leader:
Dan O'Connell came of age.

July 12th Orangemen's Parade - BELFAST.

DANIEL O'CONNELL, 1775-1847

A Kerryman, a barrister,
Who spoke like an Athenian
A Catholic loved by Protestants
(As well as proto-Fenians)
He went off to Westminster
Where he sat for County Clare,
And won emancipation for the Catholics
Fair and square.

Young Ireland backed his plan to hold
A Clontarf Monster Meeting
But Britain made him stop, and after that,
Well, fame is fleeting:
The Irish have an awful way
Of turning on their own
And in the end his former friends
Just dropped him like a stone.

ROBERT EMMETT'S "REBELLION" (1803)

An innocent, quite skilled at math
And physics and the jig
(National Jig Dance Champion
At a time when that was big).
A small man, with a smallpox face,
A charmer with no skill
At leading, organizing,
Or arousing public will.

So why the hell he ever chose
To march – 1803 –
With only eighty untrained louts,
No chance of victory?
The Crown bought off his lawyer,
His head they soon cut off,
But his last speech was great,
"Let no man write my epitaph!"

Charles Stewart Parnell, 1846-1891

A Home-Rule guy with a roving eye
Was Charles Stewart Parnell
His Land League for the tenant poor
Gave greedy landlords hell
And mobilized a thousand women,
Women who became
The suffragettes, and helped beget
What now we call Sinn Féin.

Trying to assuage her husband's rage
While bedding Kitty O'Shea
He put the man in Parliament
Where Parnell held his sway,
Until *The Times* revealed his crimes,
And then he lost his cool,
And died at forty-five
And never lived to see Home Rule.

THE GREAT FAMINE, 1845-49

A million excess deaths
And massive emigration too,
The population almost cut in half,
Poorhouses grew
To twice their size, potato harvests
Blighted, families
Just walled their cabins up and died.
All Ireland on its knees.

Some blamed it on the blight, on Britain,
Landlords, export beef,
Some said industrialization
Might have brought relief:
Ulster had it; Ulster made it;
Could the South have too?
But now most scholars just admit
They haven't got a clue.

Sir William Rowan Hamilton, 1805-1865

At thirteen years of age
His French and Arabic were good,
He also spoke some Hebrew, Persian,
Sanskrit, all he could.
When he was just eighteen years old
The Astronomer Royal said
He had become the finest
Mathematician Ireland had.

Professor of Astronomy at
The age of 22
(At Trinity), and doing
Quantum Mathematics too.
His concept the "Quaternion"
Was a radical invention,
That helped to open up the study
Of the Fourth Dimension.

GUINNESS

In 18th century Ireland
It was hard to find good beer
(And some say in the North today
It's still the same, I fear)
But one thing changed on New Years Eve
In 1759:
When Arthur Guinness bought a derelict
Brewery for a dime.

Well, 45 Pounds Sterling really,
Not too bad my dears,
Given that the lease was good
For *nine thousand years*.
Ten million pints a day are drunk
Around the world, and that's meant
A pretty good return
On Arthur Guinness's investment.

THE OLD ENGLISH
ASCENDANCY

Dublin's two cathedrals
Both St. Patrick's and Christchurch
Are Protestant, which sort of leaves
The Catholics in the lurch.
And why? They are the overwhelming
Vast majority.
Well, here we pass to that strange class
Called "The Ascendancy."

The Georgian Anglo-Irish,
To land and power bred,
"Bravado and a way with horses,"
One young poet said
With Peers, distillers, butchers,
Men with sons at Trinity
The class of Berkeley, Swift and Yeats:
That's the Ascendancy.

SANDY ROW PUBLICAN, BELFAST.
"The catholics used to know their place."

AiSLiN '75

THE SHAMROCK

Of all the Irish signs and symbols
Probably the most
Exalted is the Shamrock.
Patrick said, "The Holy Ghost,
The Father and the Son: this wee
Green three-leaf plant, you see
Shows what we mean by One and Three,
The Holy Trinity."

They say it scared the snakes away
And cured bites and stings,
But a mystery few remark upon,
Among these wondrous things,
Is something every Arab knows,
From Libya to Iraq:
A sacred three-leaf plant, in Arabic,
Is called *shamrack!*

ST. PATRICK'S CATHEDRAL: THE LADY CHAPEL

Jesus preached a lot
The last two days he was alive:
Parables and precepts
– Check out Matthew: 25.
In St. Patrick's Lady Chapel,
In stained glass, with lovely leads
Is one that really made
The poor Disciples scratch their heads.

It shows Him saying, "I was thirsty,
And ye gave me drink."
And just below the stained glass
(You'll miss it if you blink)
A small discreet brass plaque announces,
Rather modestly,
"This window is a present,
From the Guinness family."

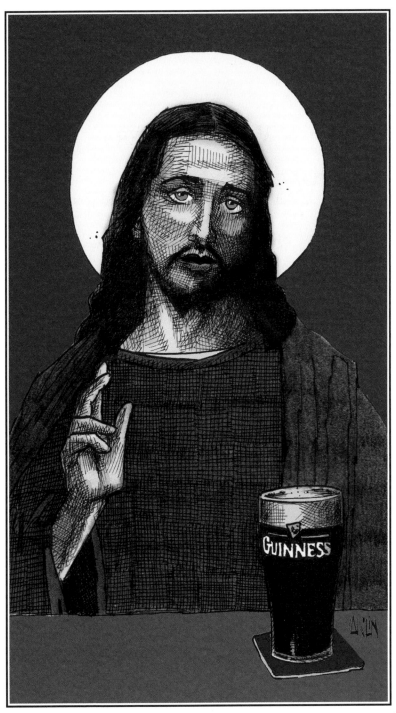

47

WATER POWER

Water power for fifteen hundred years
Had been a theme
Since horizontal paddle wheels
Were first set in a stream
To turn a pair of millstones
Grinding wheat for making bread.
It took a thousand years
Before some miller used his head

And set the mill wheel on its edge
And then two hundred more
Before J. Thomson, Queens, Belfast,
Genius to the core,
Designed a water turbine
Making electricity
In power dams, for lights and trams,
In 1883!

DUBLIN MEAN TIME (DMT) 1880

When clocks were still quite new,
And long before the pocket watch,
The towns were what you'd call
A horological hotch-potch.
Dublin was eleven minutes fast,
Compared to Cork,
Belfast: one-minute-eighteen-seconds
Off the Dublin mark.

When Dublin tries to standardize
Belfast won't go along,
And one-eighteen is still between
The Belfast clock's great gong
And Dublin's. Thirty-six more years
Go by before we see
The Belfast bong in synch along
With the world's new GMT.

LADY AUGUSTA GREGORY, 1852-1932

When she wasn't helping other
Writers night and day
She wrote herself: the Abbey Theatre
Put on forty plays,
Plays she wrote, and helped produce.
The actors spoke in these
A local dialect from Coole
She called "Kiltartanese."

When she was needed she was there,
With help and guidance, soothing,
Housing, feeding, strategizing,
Most especially schmoozing.
Without her we might not have known
Some other Irish greats
Like J.M. Synge, and Sean O'Casey,
And – especially — Yeats.

THE IRISH LITERARY THEATRE
(FOUNDED 1899)

For J.M. Synge and Sean O'Casey
It's the launching stage
That made *The Playboy*
Of the Western World a hit, a rage
Among the Dublin lit, also
The great *Plough and the Stars*.
It then became The Abbey Theatre.
In the pubs and bars

The Abbey's plays for days and days
Were studied and discussed
Helped out by many a pint and jar.
And some got really fussed
To find that, come to closing time –
(This sounds bizarre) somehow —
A few could not remember
Which wrote *Playboy*, which *The Plough*.

CONSTANCE GORE-BOOTH, COUNTESS MARKIEWICZ (1868-1927)

Ireland's first female M.P.,
The Countess Markiewicz,
A heroine to many,
But to some she was a bitch.
She joined the Irish Citizen Army,
Connelly's outfit,
But when they named her Officer,
Sean O'Casey quit.

The British sentenced her to death
After the Easter pain,
Then let her off, so she kept on,
As a member of Sinn Féin.
And Minister of Labour,
Even though she was in jail.
But even free, she never took
Her seat inside the Dáil.

MORE WOMEN OF
THE EASTER RISING

"We girls," wrote one, "set off for Stephen's
Green that day by tram."
For months they'd trained with guns, grenades,
They were *Cumann na mBan*
They met in secret, quite committed
To the use of force
To ruthlessness, to courage,
To fight without remorse.

"My house was full of rifles,
Bayonets and dynamite,"
That same one, Nora Gillies wrote,
"And also gelignite"
They fought, they died, they went to jail
They never flinched that day,
And what they started soon became
The Women's IRA.

Discussing the problems of Northern Ireland with a group of warm & open women, I found it difficult to buy myself a drink as they were very fast on the draw. Within 24 hours, the sixteen year old son of the dark haired woman (centre) was shot dead on the Falls Road by a British soldier.

OSCAR FINGAL O'FLAHERTIE WILLS WILDE: 1854-1900

When Florence Balcome jilted him
To get engaged to Bram
(Yes, *Dracula's* Bram Stoker)
Oscar took it on the lam
And lived no more in Dublin,
But won fame there anyway
With plays and novels like
The Happy Prince and *Dorian Gray*.

He lectured in America
And lived in the U.K.
Until he got two years hard labour
Just for being gay.
Jail left him broke and desolate,
He never did get well
And died of meningitis
In a dismal French hotel.

FAMOUS DUBLIN CHARACTER
(1882-1941)

He ran a cinema in Dublin,
Successfully if briefly,
Despite the booze and pubs that were
His occupation chiefly.
His fear of dogs and thunderstorms
Would leave him faint and drawn
While hanging 'round with Ezra Pound
In Paris later on

And Zurich and Trieste,
Where he was always writing stuff
Some deemed obscene, and much of which
Most readers found too tough
And yet despite his great delight
In doing all of this he's
Prob'ly best remembered for
A novel called *Ulysses*.

SAMUEL BECKETT,
1906 - 1989

A Dublin yoke whose name invokes
An almost empty stage,
His *Waiting for Godot*, a play
Became a kind of rage,
Despite the fact, one critic cracked,
(Trying to be nice)
It is a play, I have to say,
Where nothing happens . . . twice.

He took the chance and moved to France
And wrote in French, although
He also worked for Joyce (on Finnegan)
But did you know?
For his resistance role in World War II,
Few are aware
La République Française
Awarded him *La Croix de Guerre*.

WHAT THE IRISH DRINK

Whiskey isn't in it
Till the fourteenth century
And if you go back to the first
Recorded history,
Much of the early sustenance
Was blood, from bulls and cows,
Then ale and mead became
The mediaeval grand carouse.

But despite her reputation
As a nation full of boozers,
A recent European Union
Study of abusers
Showed Ireland by far
— This is the latest calculation —
Has more who totally abstain
Than any other nation.

61

WHAT THE IRISH EAT

Before the Normans came it's meat
And blood and milk and fat.
But with the great invasion there came bread
And most of that
Was wheat. There'd been some oats before
But bread was something new.
That's whole-wheat bread: you don't see white
Till 1892.[1]

There's *boxty* – bread from grated spuds,
There's *bonnyclabber* (curds),
But here's one to surprise you:
You will scarce believe my words:
The famous Irish soda bread –
Our bread – you'd never see
Until sometime well on into
The 19th century.

---

[1] (or so…)

THE IRISH AND THE JEWS

The star of Ireland's best known novel,
Is a Dublin Jew.
And anti-Semitism here
Has hurt more than a few.
But Dublin's Lord Mayor Briscoe?
(Robert), Lady Desart too?
One of the great philanthropists
The country ever knew?

The IRA burned Lady Desart's
House down, let's recall,
The story isn't finished
But it's clear, all in all,
In politics, on stage, in books,
The Irish and the Jews
Have shared a lot of values
(And have made a lot of news).

CIVIL WAR: 1920s

The treaty that at last produced
THE IRISH FREE STATE
Set brother against brother
In a fire storm of hate.
The Leader, Michael Collins,
Was ambushed and blown away
The Free State, in response,
Shot dozens, mostly IRA.

The IRA declared that they'd
Kill all TDs they'd meet
State Soldiers then tied prisoners
To a land mine in a street
Outside the Tralee jail
And lit the fuse and set it off,
Till such atrocities led all
At last to cry "Enough!"

LABOUR IN TRAVAIL, 1900-1920

Those early years in Dublin
Saw a lot of strikes and walkouts
Fights and demonstrations, rallies,
Slowdowns, even lockouts.
Biscuit-bakers, carpenters,
Box- and bottle-makers,
Electricians, engineers,
Teachers, undertakers,

Poplin workers, seamen, firemen,
Farriers, bricklayers,
Carters, cutlers, plumbers, butlers,
Even poker players.
Well – maybe that last one's a stretch,
But when you see the list
Of what those new-formed unions did
There wasn't much they missed.

JAMES LARKIN,
1876-1947

In nineteen seven, shortly after
Leaving County Down
He organized a violent dockyard strike
In Belfast Town,
In Dublin started up
The Independent Labour Party
And the Trades Union Congress.
But the most important start he

Made...the big Transport
And General Workers' lot,
Showed him the gate a few years later
Just because they thought
Him too far left.
And so he got elected to the Dáil
Where his Trades Union Act, in '43,
Crowned all that toil.

PATRICK PEARSE, 1879-1916

He runs a school for nice young boys,
And sings Cuchulain's name
And like his mythic hero
Yearns for martyrdom and fame,
But — it's only dreams, at first,
And images and words,
Until he joins the outlawed IRB[2]
And then he girds

His loins for war, and helps to form
The Irish Volunteers.
Republicans, in 1916
Vote for him, with cheers.
He's party chief in the Easter rising:
England wants him dead
And he earns his yearned-for martyrdom
When they fill him full of lead.

---

[2] The Irish Republican Brotherhood

SINN FÉIN
THEN AND NOW

Royalist Arthur Griffith founded it
In nineteen-five,
But ten years later they were broke
And only just alive.
In 1916 Britain blamed
Sinn Féin for those events,
— A lie, they'd stayed away —
But De Valera saw his chance.

In '17 he took it,
Used the Easter reputation
To build it – in one year
To sweep the vote throughout the nation.
In harness with the IRA today
It seems to thrive,
Without a trace of what took place
In nineteen-hundred five.

JOHN BUTLER YEATS, 1839-1922

He said to sitters, "You can't see it,
It's not finished," still he
Finally let the family see
His heads of Jack and Willy
Luminous portraits of his sons
That still, in any light'll
Leave a critic mute or gasping,
"Stunning, brilliant, vital!"

And so, while hundreds more were stored
Where none could ever see 'em,
We knew some day they'd make their way
To every great museum
And bring those names to lasting fame
Of everyone who sits . . .
But, sadly, most were lost to bombs
In London, in the Blitz.

W. B. YEATS, 1869-1939

On lives and loves and liberties,
And destinies and fates
There's none so fine with a rhyming line
As William Butler Yeats.
Some said he was a fascist,
But that's a pack of lies
They'd never give a fascist
The bloody Nobel Prize.

There is a pub in Sligo
Where everybody eats.
It's named for Bill, and there they still
Refer to him as "Yeets."
His gravestone's just across the way,
But the Verger there maintains
That they brought the wrong box home from France,
And it isn't his remains.

GEORGE BERNARD SHAW, 1856-1950

Arms and the Man, Candida, Barbara,
Man and Superman,
You Never Can tell, Back to Methuselah,
Pygmalion.
Socialist, eugenicist,
Strict vegetarian
An eager motorcyclist,
He gave another man

The bike that killed him — T. E. Lawrence —
(Which was really sadder
Than Shaw's own death at 94
From falling off a ladder.)
The only person in one lifetime
Ever to have won
Both an Oscar (My Fair Lady)
And the Nobel Prize (Saint Joan).

73

ALICE MILLIGAN, 1866- 1953

A poet and an editor,
A friend of Yeats and Gonne
She fought for Ireland's independence,
Some would say she won
(Or helped to win)
Because she thought that language, art, and writing
On pride and freedom were worth more
Than politics and fighting.

She started up a weekly mag in Belfast
Shan Van Vocht
On Doing-It Ourselves, it made
The Powers quite provoked.
And so when freedom came
Was Alice famed among the many?
Well, no, she died, in Omagh, home,
Alone, without a penny.

Elizabeth Bowen,
1899-1972

Bowen's Court in County Cork,
The Country House where she
Grew up to be about as Irish
As a girl could be,
Until she moved to England
And became a novelist
But then came home in World War Two
And gave her life a twist

By sending London secret briefs
About neutrality
And Irish pride and stubbornness
And the Ascendancy.
Well, after that life went downhill,
Elizabeth went bust
And when she died great Bowens Court
Was smashed and left in dust.

PART II

THE STONES

THE GREAT FORESTS

Back thirteen hundred centuries
The landbridge brought in deer
And grass and wolves and seeds and trees
And for ten thousand years
Ireland was home to birch
And juniper, and pine
Elm, oak, hazel, willow, cedar —
Wood of every kind.

Then humans came, and cut and split
And burned and built and sold
Casks and beams and ships, to Britain —
That brought in the gold.
But iron smelting was what did
The forests in at last,
And Ireland's now the thinnest wooded
Country Europe has.

A GEOLOGICAL WONDER

Beneath the vast flat calcite shelf
Just off the northwest shore,
Sixty million years ago
There heaved up from the core
A trillion tons of molten lava
Turning all that ocean
Into a boiling cauldron
That stayed in constant motion

For centuries until the basalt
Cooling from top down
Formed forty thousand pillars, flat-topped
Gleaming lustrous brown.
Today on weekends its quite often
Uncle's, Dad's or Ma's way
To entertain the kids
By showing them The Giant's Causeway.

THE RUNES: PREHISTORY

The glaciers retreating
Thirty thousand years ago
Left what we call The Irish Sea
Landlocked, to take the flow
From all that ice, and possibly –
Landlocked both south and north —
Was still a vast fresh water lake,
When humans first came forth.

Around its shores, five thousand years ago
Carved stones appear,
Runic spirals set on tombs,
Forms that still endure
Across the aeons, stone age, bronze age,
On the early crosses,
Churches, banks, wherever folk
Recorded gains and losses.

THE POULNABRONE

Near Caherconnel, County Clare
This dolmen's limestone cairn
Enclosed the crumbling bones of thirty
Humans, one a bairn
A few months old: a polished axe,
A scraper, beads and shards
Some arrowheads and other flints
Within this place that guards

A host of ancient secrets
Giving form to this strange tomb.
What ritual? What purpose?
What race? Whence had they come?
By sea? Across the landbridge?
How can we ever know
What shades, what lights, what dreads they shared
Three thousand years ago.

WOLVES

The oldest eoliths show wolves
In forests west to east
Feeding at first on deer and then
On every kind of beast
The early farmers raised,
And so of course the men began
To kill the wolves. (It's neat to note
Wolves never killed a man.)

Something like eight hundred
Was the most they'd ever counted.
Oliver Cromwell felled a million trees
And then he mounted
A total war on wolves.
But hunters only found a few
And they shot the very last one dead
In 1762.

THE ROUND FORTS

There's thousands of them, some a berm
A moat and not much more,
But some so vast they make the old
Imagination soar.
There's one near Letterkenny
It's early iron age,
They say, it's got 13 foot walls,
Internal stairs, a page

Of history that so far
Is only dimly known
Rebuilt around AD 500
By The O'Neill, in stone.
The King of Munster wrecked it.
Modern scholars built it back
To what O'Neill had named
The Grianan of Aileach.

QUEEN MAEVE

A legendary cairn in Sligo
Some ten metres tall,
And fifty-five across;
Is said to be the grave where all
That's left of Maeve of Connaght
Was laid. She was the queen
Who fought Cuchulain for The Bull
Of Ulster, which was deemed

To be the only one that would
Allow brave Maeve to claim
Equal status with her man —
(King Ailill was his name.)
She brought it home to meet her husband's
Bull, and thought she'd won,
But the two bulls killed each other
Leaving Maeve back at square one.

PART III

SOME IRISH URBAN LEGENDS

DERRY
(CONTROVERSIALLY, "LONDONDERRY")

Old Derry's had more troubles, see,
Than any other place
(Well, the Irish have been living there
Since the founding of the race.)
Viking swoops and British troops,
And then the Nine Years War
And sixteen-eight, O'Dogherty
Wipes out the Brits once more,

The Long Siege, the Bogside,
The Union, I.R.A.
And Bloody Sunday (nineteen-seventy-two)
The blackest day –
And yet despite the endless strife
It recently was voted
One of the ten best UK towns to live in.
— Duly noted.

A solitary pub still stands in DERRY, the Bogside,
just a few yards from the sight of Bloody Sunday.

THE CITY OF CORK (6ᵀᴴ C. TO NOW)

Well it's a shame to tie its name
To whiskey, beer, and drunks
This brilliant port that got its start
As a colony of monks.
The town survived the Black Death twice
And other acts of God
The Huguenots arrived in droves
(The place was mostly Prod.)

The English made it rich with trade
In iron, wool and wine,
The College and the railway came
In 1849
Ten thousand peasants fled the famine
Here to seek a shilling
And – truth to say – Cork still makes hay
From brewing and distilling.

DUNGLOE

At Dungloe, County Donegal
A gathering each year
Brings Irish girls called Mary
Round the world, from far and near.
"The Festival of the Marys,"
Song and dance — and TV stars —
It's such a rout it empties out
A lot of pubs and bars.

Dungloe was *An Clochan Lia'th*
Until the monthly fair
Was moved from *Dun an Gleo'*
Five miles north, to Rosses, where
They now run schools and make the rules
And sell food, beer and soap
Through a Rosses district supermarket chain
They call *The Cope*.

THE TOWN OF KILLYBEGS

It's just about as far west
As you'll get in Donegal.
The name suggests you'd never
Take it serious at all.
Well, wrong: there's sometimes sixty trawlers
Docked here at one time.
Pelagic fish, tons, frozen,
Shipped to every land and clime.

Windmill parts arrive here too
(Wind power's very big
In Ireland, and the harbour's deep
Enough for any rig).
And Killybegs famed carpets, "Donegals,"
Are walked upon
By princes, popes, and presidents
From Rome to Washington.

WATERFORD CITY, 914 AD

"Urbs Intacta Manet Waterfordia"

"*The City Never Taken*" is its motto,
But in fact
The Irish took it from the Danes,
The Danes then took it back,
And then MacMorrough, King of Leinster,
Brought a Norman Earl
From England, Strongbow was his name,
And *they* gave it a whirl.

So by 1170
It's Ireland's second city,
In 1783 the glassworks,
Now they're sitting pretty
A major port, shipbuilding too,
And some say Best of all,
A doughy bun affectionately
Known today as 'Blaa.

HARLAND AND WOLFF

Harland and Wolff, the shipyards,
Hitler's target in Belfast.
Two hundred Junkers 88's
Came in one night. The blast
Left tens of thousands homeless,
Killed a thousand, knocked down half
The buildings. (They'd just *seven* Ack-Ack guns.
No RAF.)

The first keel laid, in 1870,
Was the *Oceanic*,
And later one we all recall, of course,
The doomed *Titanic*.
Today the gantries, Samson
And Goliath, doze: no boats
Are built where that great dry-dock
Could hold anything that floats.

LETTERKENNY,
17TH CENTURY

Letterkenny got a lift
With Punts and the first banks,
Probably the only things
Back then that earned their thanks
Out of the great Partition,
In the 1920s there,
Which at the start gave many folk
In Donegal a scare.

But with the money came a boom
In services and art
And businesses and all the things
That money helps to start.
Now: some still give the credit
To a yoke called St. Conal
For the first big spurt was Conal's
Psychiatric Hospital

97

GALWAY CITY, 1241 AD

"The Town of Fourteen Tribes," they said.
But only two were Celt
A bay that's great for oysters, herring,
Mackerel, shrimp and smelt,
A Catholic fort, a vital port
For French and Spanish wine
Till 1652 when Cromwell
Held it siege for nine

Long months, and then it was
Quite Protestant, until
It turned again with James's men
And fought against King Bill.
Today, (perhaps this is a sign
Of what such things entail)
A fine Cathedral sits
On what was once the City Gaol.

SHANNON

To the envy of Cork City,
Work began in '36
To build a giant runway here,
An airport that would fix
The transatlantic gateway problem.
Flights both from and to
Europe, UK, America,
Began in '42.

They drained the bogs, it has few fogs,
Aer Lingus got a boost,
And *all* the airlines used it
As a temporary roost.
But the aspect that transformed
The whole world's travel history?
Well! Shannon was the world's first airport
That was duty-free.

THE EMIGRANTS

Around the world there must be
Twenty million, maybe more,
In London, Paris, New York Boston
Beirut, Singapore,
Driven out by weather, debt or neighbours
(Once they've written
Their sentimental memoirs
It will all be blamed on Britain.)

A cultural force from pole to pole
In commerce and the arts
That's left its mark on our imaginations
And our hearts.
But *emigrant* seems kind of dry:
The greatness of it calls for a
New word: Mary Robinson's:
"Our Diaspora."

THE CELTIC TIGER,
(1985 . . . OR SO)

That's what they call the great financial boom
That hit the place
After Ireland joined
The European Union's race
To be the economic giant
Of the world, a spin
That soon saw Euros by the tens
Of billions pouring in.

But dependent-earner ratios
Are what makes a country's wealth
And once the Catholic Church no longer ruled,
The birth rate fell.
So perhaps it's not the Euro
That's made Ireland look so regal,
But the laws of 1985
When they made condoms legal.